For Sophie

THE HEDGEHOG'S PRICKLY PROBLEM!

DON CONROY

THE O'BRIEN PRESS
DUBLIN

This revised and redesigned edition first published 1995
by The O'Brien Press Ltd.,
20 Victoria Road, Rathgar, Dublin 6, Ireland.
Reprinted 1996 (twice), 1998
First edition published 1992.
Copyright text and illustrations © Don Conroy

BRITISH LIBRARY CATALOGUING-IN-PUBLICATION DATA
Conroy, Don
Hedgehog's Prickly Problem!
I. Title
823.914 [J]

The O'Brien Press receives
assistance from

The Arts Council
An Chomhairle Ealaíon

ISBN 0-86278-415-8

4   6   8   10   9   7   5
98 00 02 04 03 01 99

Cover illustration: Don Conroy
Cover design: O'Brien Press
Cover separations: Lithoset, Dublin
Printing: Cox & Wyman Ltd., Reading

Harry Hedgehog was bored.
He rolled into a ball and tried a
few tumbles in the grass. But when he
unfolded he was still bored.

'I'M BORED! BORED! BORED!' he
yelled, but nobody answered. A bee
just buzzed by.

'What will I do?' he said to himself.
But he could think of nothing. Maybe
my friend Otus could help, he thought.
I'll go and ask him about it. And he
shuffled off.

High up in the scots pine tree, Otus, the long-eared owl, was dozing. It was warm and sunny. He sat very still, his body pressed against the bark of the tree.

His feathers looked just like the tree trunk, and no-one would notice him unless they looked very hard – especially not the magpies! They were *such* a nuisance!

Otus settled himself for a long, comfortable rest. Then he heard tapping. Otus blinked and opened his eyes. A man stood at the tree, hammering something on to it.

'What's this?' said Otus to himself.

He waited. When the man left, Otus checked for traps or wires, but all he could see was a bit of paper stuck to the trunk of the tree.

'Looks safe enough,' he
muttered, and down he swept
to have a look.

It was a big notice with pictures of
lions, tigers, sealions, elephants and
horses, and men dressed in funny
clothes.

'What's this?' he said again.

There was a shuffling in the
undergrowth.

That sounds like Harry Hedgehog, thought Otus, and, sure enough, the hedgehog moved out into the clearing.

'Well, Harry,' said Otus cheerfully, 'how are you this morning?'

'Actually,' Harry said, 'I'm bored.'

'BORED!' Otus laughed. 'I think I was bored once, a long time ago –'

'Once! Really! What did you do? I can't think of anything.' Harry looked miserable.

'Went to sleep! And when I woke up it was gone,' announced Otus. 'Simple as that!'

Harry didn't look convinced. 'What is boredom anyway?' he asked. 'I know what it feels like, but what is it?'

'Well,' said the owl wisely, 'it's like a cloud passing over the sun and stopping the sunshine.

'But after a
time it passes
and we have
sunshine again. Then
everything is all right.'

'You're very clever,'
said Harry. 'I never knew
the sun got bored!'

'Oh dear!' said Otus. 'I don't think
you fully grasped my meaning.'

'What's going on?' came another
voice. It was Sammy Squirrel. He
leaped down the tree, looking
anything but bored.

Harry started to explain, but Sammy wasn't listening. 'Hey, look!' he said. 'Who put this here?' He pointed to the poster.

'A man came and pinned it to the tree,' said Otus.

Harry came closer to see it too, although he couldn't see very much from the ground. 'What does it mean?' he asked. Already he had forgotten about being bored.

'Looks like a circus,' suggested Otus.

'I wonder when it's coming?' said Sammy.

'Well, the one who'll be able to tell us is Old Lepus. He knows everything there is to know,' said Otus.

'I'll go and get him,' said Sammy, and off he went.

The other woodland friends arrived. There was Bentley Badger, Renny Fox and Ollie Otter, and they all sat around staring at the poster. 'Pity we can't read it,' sighed Otus.

'Maybe these animals have gone missing,' suggested Bentley. 'And those men in strange clothes want them back.'

'I don't think so,' said Renny. 'The men look far too happy for that.'

Old Lepus, the wise old hare, arrived with Sammy. 'What's all the excitement?' he asked.

'Look!' said Otus, pointing to the poster. 'What does it mean?'

'Let me see,' said the old hare, as he took out his glasses and cleaned them. Then he held them to his eyes and began to read:

**THE GREAT CALLINO CIRCUS
IS COMING TO TOWN!
WE ARE LOOKING FOR NEW ACTS
FOR OUR NATIONWIDE TOUR
ANIMAL PERFORMERS
ESPECIALLY WELCOME
AUDITIONS WILL TAKE PLACE
1 JUNE (ALL DAY) IN OUR BIG TOP**

'New acts!' said Harry Hedgehog. 'Animal performers! *I'm* an animal – I could perform. Then I wouldn't be bored any more!' He began to perform there and then, rolling into a ball ...

But nobody was watching, because just then Billy Blackbird arrived, shouting loudly.

'What's up?' asked Sammy Squirrel.

'I've just seen a lot of strange animals in cages!' announced Billy. 'Huge animals.'

'That must be the circus!' said Old Lepus.

'And there's a big striped tent in a field near Malone's farm.'

'Let's all go and take a look,' suggested Otus.

Old Lepus couldn't join them. 'There's an injured sparrowhawk coming to see me this morning. But do come around for supper this evening and tell me all about it,' he said.

Everyone was delighted with this –
supper with Old Lepus was always a
treat.

'Be careful,' warned Old Lepus as he
set off for his home. 'Don't do
anything foolish!'

The woodland friends ran off to Malone's farm, and there stood the biggest tent they had ever seen. It was taller than the trees and seemed to go up into the clouds!

'Wow!' said Harry.

'We'd better make sure we're not seen,' warned Renny. So they stood behind the hedgerow to look.

Men and women were busy pulling on ropes and hammering stakes into the ground. There was one man who looked almost as tall as the tent itself and he walked around slowly, gazing down on everyone. One group of people climbed on top of each other and made a star shape.

Then they saw large cages on
wheels. A lion paced up and down in
one of the cages while its mate sat in
the corner yawning.

'Hey!' called Harry. 'Look at those
funny horses with stripes all over them!'

'Those are zebras, silly,' said Bentley Badger. 'From Africa.'

'Look over there!' said Harry again. 'That's definitely the biggest worm I've ever seen.'

Billy Blackbird was at his side in a shot – Billy was *very* interested in worms, especially huge ones. 'Where? Where?' he asked, his voice high with excitement.

'Look! Wrapped around that woman over there,' said Harry.

'That's a snake,' said Renny Fox. 'A python, I think. Old Lepus showed me one once –'

'He showed you a snake!' gasped Harry.

'Not a *real* one, silly,' said Renny. 'A picture of one.'

They saw a man jumping backwards, tumbling over and over and then landing on his feet. He did this again and again, and sometimes landed on his back instead.

'I could easily do that,' Sammy Squirrel scoffed. 'Watch.'

'Not now,' warned Otus. 'We don't want to get caught. We might all end up in the circus!'

'You have to have talent to be in a circus,' said Harry proudly.

'How would you know?' said Sammy.

'I just do!' snapped Harry.

Two dogs who were chained to a caravan started to bark loudly. 'They must have picked up our scent,' said Renny Fox. 'Let's get out of here. See you all at Old Lepus's this evening.'

They all raced off in different directions, but Harry hid under the hedgerow for a while, gazing longingly at the circus. It was all so new and exciting.

On his way home, Harry passed by two horses grazing in a field.

'I have news for you!' Harry told them. 'Did you know you have cousins who are all black with white stripes ... or is it all white with black stripes? And they come from Africa!' Wherever that is, he thought to himself.

The horses looked at each other as Harry shuffled off, pleased with himself.

'What do you make of that?' said one horse to the other.

'I'd say a bit too much of the sun,' said the other. 'Everyone knows our cousins are chestnut and that they live on the Curragh racecourse.' They laughed about it all day.

✳   ✳   ✳

'Well, tell me about the circus,' said Old Lepus, as he brought out delicious pies and cool spring water for supper. They all sat around, munching.

'It was fantastic!' said Ollie. 'All those unusual animals – elephants, sealions, tigers ...'

'I suppose,' Bentley butted in, 'they're unusual only because we've never seen them before. Maybe *we* look unusual to them.'

'Very true,' laughed Old Lepus. 'What I like most about a circus is the clowns ...'

And they talked all evening about the wonders of the circus. The moon was out before they all trooped off home.

＊　＊　＊

Harry Hedgehog shuffled along slowly towards his bed. Now, what was it that was bothering me this morning? Oh yes, I was bored. Oh no, why did I have to remind myself?

He sat on a tree stump, his head in his paws. 'BORED! BORED! How annoying,' he said.

Suddenly there was a loud shriek, and Barny Owl flew down to him.

Harry jumped in fright. '*Must* you make such a loud noise?' he exclaimed. 'I nearly jumped out of my skin.'

'Oh, don't be so grumpy,' said Barny. 'What's the matter with you?'

'I'm bored,' said Harry.

'What?'

'Bored. You know,
like when a cloud lands on you and
won't go away.'

'That's called FOG,' said Barny.

Harry folded his arms and looked
glum.

'Were you like this all day?' asked
Barny.

'Only in the morning,' said Harry
gloomily, 'and now.'

'Then something happened in the middle of the day that made you happy!'

'Yes! That's it. You're a genius, Barny,' said Harry, all excited now.

The owl stared back blankly.

'The circus, of course!' beamed Harry. 'That's what I'll do – I'll join the circus. Then I'll be happy all the time, never bored. And I'll be famous.'

Harry was leaping around with excitement now. 'Ah yes, the smell of the crowd and the roar of the greasepaint –' he stopped, something wrong there, but what?

'Who cares!' he yelled. He gave
Barny a big hug. 'Goodbye, Barny, old
pal, I'm off to join the circus. Say
goodbye to everyone for me and come
visit me sometime. I'll still talk to
everyone even when I'm
famous. It won't go to my
head, I promise!
Goodbye!'

And off he went as quick as his little hedgehog legs could carry him, through the ferns towards Malone's farm.

Barny waved goodbye after him, not sure what to think. He was happy that Harry was happy, but sad to see him go. He hoped he *would* become famous and that he'd be happy with circus life.

* * *

Harry stopped to sleep beside a beech tree, tucked snugly into one of the smooth roots growing above ground. He slept soundly all night, having wonderful dreams about the

Big Top. He could hear the ringmaster, in his top hat and red jacket, blowing his whistle and shouting loudly: 'Ladies and gentlemen, boys and girls, Callino's Circus is proud to present – Harry the Hedgehog!' Then Harry would come out into the ring, the spotlight shining on him, and he would bow as the crowd cheered.

The roar of a lion woke Harry.

Wow! he thought, I suppose I'll have to get used to that sound. He set off down the hill towards the Big Top. 'Fame and fortune wait for me,' he sang happily. Suddenly slipping on the dewy grass, he went into a spin and rolled all the way down, gathering speed on the way. He bounced several times like a ball, and didn't stop until he reached a row of people and animals, all queuing up to audition in front of the circus owner and the ringmaster. Harry came to an abrupt halt when he hit the leg of the table where the circus men sat.

Everyone started to shout:

'Hey! There's a queue here.'

'Some of us have been waiting all night.'

'Get back to the end of the line.'

But the circus men ignored them all.
'Not bad!' said the owner to the
ringmaster, looking in surprise at
Harry. 'But a poor finish. You need to
work on your act,' he said to Harry.

Harry sat on the gound looking at
the stars spinning around in his head,
unable to speak.

'The waistcoat is a novel idea,' said
the owner. 'Could be a class act.'

'Name?' asked the ringmaster.

Harry dusted himself off. 'Harry
Hedgehog. I wish to join the circus,' he
announced.

'What was that?' asked the owner.
'Can anyone speak hedgehog?'

Everyone shook their heads. A snake slithered off a woman's shoulder and hissed at Harry: 'Clear off! There are much more important acts here – especially me.'

Harry trembled. 'Yes, worm ... I mean er ... em ... snake.'

'We'll see if we can find a spot for you,' said the ringmaster. 'Wait over there.' He pointed.

Harry moved aside quickly, away from the snake and the other angry faces.

'At least *he* understands *us*,' said the circus owner.

Harry's career in the circus was about to begin, but he was worried and puzzled. I thought people in the circus were supposed to be happy, he thought to himself. I hope it was a good idea to come.

❋   ❋   ❋

Back in the woods Renny Fox was worried. He couldn't find Harry *anywhere*. He searched and called, but there was no sign of his little friend.

Renny called on Sammy Squirrel and Ollie Otter. 'Anyone seen Harry? He's been gone for days.'

'No,' they both said.

Along came Bentley Badger shuffling through the undergrowth. 'Anything up? You all look worried.'

'Well,' explained Renny, 'nobody has seen Harry for days.'

'Maybe Barny would
know where he is,'
suggested Bentley.
They ran to Barny's castle.
'Barny! Barny!' they yelled.
There was no answer.
'Nobody home,' said Renny.

But just then Barny swooped down.
He gave a screech of welcome,
delighted to see all his friends. They all
jumped in fright.

'Have you seen Harry?' asked Ollie.

'Yes,' said Barny. 'I flew over to check on him. He's working really hard, so I didn't disturb him, I just watched from a distance ...'

'Working? Barny, where *is* he?' asked Renny.

'With the circus,' explained Barny.

'The *circus!*' They were all shocked.

'You mean he's left the woods?' Renny said. 'Forever?'

'Yes,' said Barny. 'He told me to say goodbye to everyone and that we should visit him sometime. He was bored, you know, he wanted to do something different.'

Harry was doing something different all right. The going was very tough at the circus. He just never seemed to get anything right. The very first morning he was told to blow up a hundred balloons for the afternoon show. He blew and blew and blew until he was blue in the face, but every single balloon hit against his prickles and burst!

One of the clowns came by and saw the difficulty. 'I'll blow those up for you,' he offered, and he did. Then he gave a pile of them to Harry, tied together on a string. Harry grasped the balloons, and just then a gust of wind blew and lifted the poor hedgehog right off his feet and up into the air. He ended up stuck in a tree.

'Help! Help!' he yelled. The stiltman had to get him down. His next job was to wash the elephants. This went fine until he turned the water pressure up too high and the hose jerked about like a crazy snake.

Everyone was drenched, all the fancy
costumes soaked. And then water
splashed into an elephant's eye.
The elephant picked Harry up
in its trunk and threw
him up in the air.

He went flying over the cages,
through the open window of the
owner's caravan – and landed right in
the owner's soup! Splash! The circus
owner jumped with fright. His
face went bright red with
anger.

'I suppose I'm really
in the soup now,'
said Harry.

Luckily the owner did not understand. He gave a loud roar. 'You! You're more trouble than you're worth! Get out of my sight.'

Harry climbed quickly out of the soup.

'Out!' shouted the owner again, pointing to the window.

Harry leapt out the window and scurried away. He decided to hide for a while until things cooled down. He'd have a snooze – a sleep always made things better. He crept into a quiet tent and closed his eyes.

What Harry didn't realise was that he was in the trapeze artist's tent. The trapeze man was having a rest too before the afternoon show. They both slept soundly, then the trapeze man got up and began to exercise, stretching his muscles, bending over ...

'Ouch! Ow! Ow!' he yelled suddenly in a shrill voice.

The ringmaster arrived to see the trapeze man hopping around the tent holding one foot and screaming. 'My foot! My foot!'

'What's this?' Some kind of new act?' asked the ringmaster.

'No!' snapped the trapeze man. 'There's something terribly sharp down there – I don't know what it can be. I keep this place spick and span ...'

The ringmaster looked and saw Harry still curled up asleep. He grabbed him by the waistcoat and held him up. 'Could this be the culprit?'

It was, of course.

The ringmaster marched off to the circus owner's caravan to explain what had happened – Antonio was unable to do his trapeze act because of a foot injury. The owner was furious.

'And this is the
cause of it all,' said the
ringmaster, holding
Harry out towards the owner.

'You! Again!' yelled the owner.

Harry tried to smile. 'Have I done
something wrong?'

The circus owner glared back.

'A circus is not a circus without a trapeze act,' shouted the owner. '*You* will do the trapeze act tonight. You will walk on the tight rope, you WILL NOT FALL. If you do ...' The owner drew his finger along his neck from ear to ear.

Harry didn't know what this meant,
but he did know it wasn't good.

That evening they put a red and gold
cloak on Harry, then the ringmaster
blew his whistle and in a loud voice
announced a great new discovery:
'Spikino the Hedgehog, the World's
Only Hedgehog Tightrope Walker!'

The audience clapped and cheered
as Harry entered the ring. Arms
outstretched, he walked to the centre,
and bowed gracefully.

Now in the audience was one very special guest. It was Sammy Squirrel. He had sneaked under the canvas and crept to the back of the seats to see the show. And here was his friend Harry in a classy act! Sammy was so proud of him.

I must go back and tell the others right away not to worry. Harry is fine – and he's famous, Sammy thought, and off he raced, full of excitement with his great news.

✳   ✳   ✳

Harry began to climb the rope ladder to the cheers of the crowd. As he went higher and higher he began to feel nervous. The people disappeared farther and farther into the distance. Was this such a good idea after all?

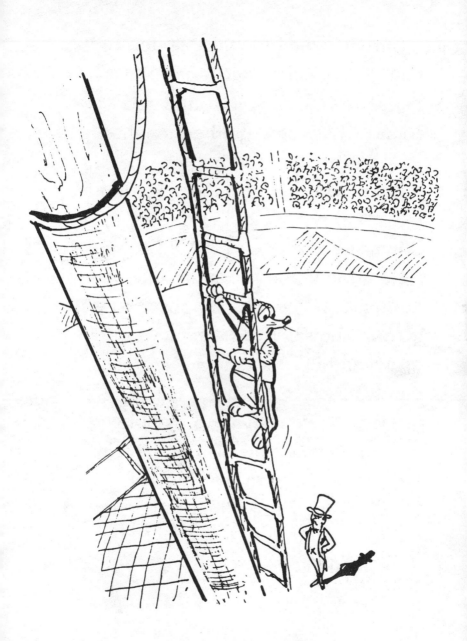

Harry reached the very tip top of the tent. He looked down – and the people began to spin round and round. That's strange, he thought, they'll get so dizzy – but then he saw the poles spinning round and round too. 'Oops!' he yelled. 'I mustn't look down.'

He gripped the ladder and looked at the tightrope he was supposed to walk across. The safety net seemed very far away, and in between was a huge empty space.

Harry's knees began to wobble.

Then he made up his mind. I'll just have to do it, he said to himself, there's no way out. I'll just pretend I'm out for a stroll in the woods. Nothing to be afraid of.

The crowd watched and waited, straining their eyes to see the little figure way above their heads.

'Here goes!' said Harry, and he stepped gingerly onto the wire. It began to sway from side to side.

Harry stopped. Maybe I could go back to blowing balloons, he thought. But he noticed the owner waving his fist at him.

Harry bent down and crawled carefully on all fours along the rope. He was getting confident now – this wasn't too bad after all.

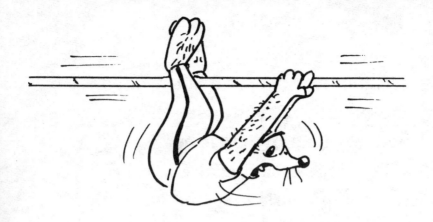

Then suddenly he found himself swinging upside down, holding on for dear life! Wow! How did that happen? he wondered.

He tried to swing his body back up onto the rope again. After a few goes he got there.

The crowd was cheering loudly and Harry perked up. I wonder could I manage it standing up? he thought. There's only one way to find out.

Carefully, he stood up, put out his arms for balance, and moved forward, one foot at a time. 'Hey! I'm doing it,' he shouted, though nobody could hear him. 'I'm tightrope walking! If only my friends could see me. I wonder could Sammy do this? I don't think so. Only the Great Harry Spikino the Tightrope-walking Hedgehog can do it.'

Harry was feeling very confident now. He got half-way along the rope.

Everything was going fine until he looked down at the audience again. Then it all began to spin round and round once more.

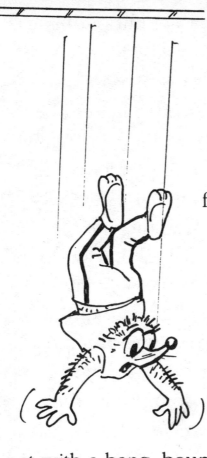

'Oh no! Wow! Help ...' and with that he fell head first down towards the ground. Harry closed his eyes and waited for the worst. He rolled himself into a ball as tight as could be. He hit the safety net with a bang, bounced out again high in the air way up over the audience – and landed right in the candyfloss machine!

Opening one eye Harry saw pink clouds. Then he opened the other. More pink clouds. Am I in heaven? he wondered. He pushed the 'clouds' apart. Wow, they're sticky, he thought. He licked his hand. But they taste great! Strange, I never knew clouds were like this.

He began to eat his way out of the candyfloss until he came to something solid. Then he walked around the inside of the machine. No way out!

This is a strange kind of heaven, thought Harry. Sort of *small*. Maybe it's not heaven at all, maybe it's ... maybe it's ... Just then hands reached into the candyfloss and a stick was poked through towards Harry.

'Grab that stick,' said the circus owner's voice sternly.

Oh no! Not him again! thought Harry. But he caught the stick and was pulled out of the machine.

The owner had the same look on his face as when Harry had fallen into his soup – dark, cross and threatening. But he put on a false smile for the audience and walked quickly out of

the Big Top with Harry swinging from his cane over his shoulder. The crowd clapped and clapped. They must have thought this was all part of the act – a clowning hedgehog acrobat!

'That's very nice pink stuff!' Harry said. 'You should sell that, you know. People would definitely buy it ...'

The owner said nothing. He plonked Harry in a cage, shut the door and left.

That evening the owner and other circus members sat at a table wondering what they should do with the hedgehog. Harry was placed on the table in front of them.

The ringmaster suggested he could be a prickly cannonball and be shot out of the cannon. The sealion tamer thought he could be a great ball for the sealions to play with. The clowns didn't want him anywhere near their act in case he got all the laughs. They argued all evening.

Finally, the knife thrower pointed his
sharp knife at Harry. 'Why don't we do
what the gypsies did long ago with
hedgehogs?' He sniggered, flashing his
big white teeth.

'An excellent idea!' said the circus
owner, and they all agreed.

'I don't agree!' Harry said, but
nobody understood. He didn't have
any idea what was going to happen,
but he knew it didn't sound good.

'That's settled, then,' said the circus owner. 'Lock him up in that birdcage again until tomorrow – just in case he tries to escape.'

Harry was put back into the small cage.

'Sleep well, now,' said the owner. 'Tomorrow we have just the act for you.'

Back in the woods Sammy had called the friends together to tell them how well Harry was doing at the circus.

'They call him Spikino the Hedgehog,' he announced.

'Wow!' said Renny. 'Sounds great!'

'I suppose he's not ever bored now,' said Otus, the long-eared owl. 'He must be far too busy.'

'Well, I miss him already and he's only gone a few days,' sighed Bentley Badger.

'Pity we couldn't give him a farewell party,' said Barny.

They all agreed.

'Why don't we have a party to celebrate his success?' suggested Renny.

Everyone was thrilled with this idea and they started to work out a plan.

Just then Billy Blackbird arrived. 'Hey
everyone!' he chirped. 'What's
happening?'

'We're planning a party for Harry,'
explained Bentley. 'To celebrate his
success.'

'Too late!' announced Billy. 'The
circus has gone, and Harry's gone
with it.'

'Gone!' they all exclaimed together.

'Yes,' said Billy. 'I saw them take down the Big Top, put all the animals in cages and leave.'

'Oh!' said Sammy. 'What will we do now? We *must* see Harry before he's too far away for us to visit him. Let's go!'

They headed off in search of the circus. In the field where the Big Top had stood there were only torn posters and litter on the ground. Then Barny noticed something and swooped down to take a closer look. He gave a loud shriek.

'What is it?' asked Renny.

'Look! Look!' Barny said, calling them over to the object on the ground. Bentley picked it up. It was Harry's waistcoat.

'That was a birthday present from Old Lepus,' said Sammy. 'Harry would never leave that behind. He must be in trouble.'

'The circus is getting farther away by the minute. Let's go!' said Otus.

Renny snapped into action. 'Otus, you and Billy and Barny should fly ahead and try to locate the circus. We'll all follow along as quickly as we can.'

They set off, and Barny gave Sammy a lift on his back while Otus and Billy flew beside them. They all kept a sharp look out.

It was nearly dusk when they came upon the circus trucks and carriages. The trailers with the elephants and zebras were being pulled by horses. Barny and Sammy sailed over them. A leopard growled from one of the cages. But there was no sign of Harry.

Then they heard a voice: 'Hi, guys!'

'Did you hear that?' said Barny. 'That sounded just like Harry.'

They flew round and round, but Harry was nowhere to be seen.

Suddenly everything came to a halt. The trucks and caravans pulled into a field and formed a circle. A huge fire was lit and everyone sat around, chatting and eating. They were to stay here for the night.

From the trees Otus, Barny and Sammy waited for their friends to arrive. Billy had flown back to tell them where to go.

At last they saw Renny and Ollie making their way across the fields with Bentley puffing and panting behind.

'Any sign of Harry?' asked Renny.

'We thought we heard him, but we couldn't see any sign of him,' said Barny.

'That's strange,' said Ollie. 'What'll we do?'

'When things get quiet, we'll sneak over and look around,' said Renny.

'Maybe only one of us should go. If
we get caught then at least only one
is trapped,' said Otus.

'Good thinking,' agreed Renny.
'Let's pull straws.'

They pulled pieces of grass and compared sizes. Sammy's was the shortest.

'Okay, I'm the one,' he said. He seemed pleased. Barny said he'd fly overhead and help.

'Good luck,' they all said as Sammy crept under the fence and headed towards the campfire.

Men and women sat around drinking and singing and chatting. There was no sign of Harry.

Sammy passed by a cage where four lions slept soundly. He wondered should he wake them and ask about Harry. He thought maybe not. A large python in a glass case opened one green eye, then moved its body up along the glass. 'Looking for something?' the snake asked.

Sammy stopped and stared. He was amazed by this strange creature. He had never seen a snake before.

'Why don't you take the lid off and climb in here?' the snake said slyly. 'It's nice and warm. And maybe I can help you.'

Sammy put his paws on the top of the glass and was just about to slide it across when he heard a loud shriek. It was Barny.

'Don't do that!' he
shrieked louder. 'That snake
only wants you for a nice meal!'
   The snake hissed in annoyance.
   Two men appeared, flashing a torch
around the ground. Barny flapped
away.

'Only a white owl!' said one man, switching off his torch. 'Nothing to worry about. Let's get back to the card game.'

Sammy stayed hidden until things settled down again. That was a near miss! he thought. I must be more careful. Lucky for me Barny was watching.

He thought he heard a familiar voice. That really does sound like Harry, thought Sammy. He must be near.

There were some horses grazing in long grass behind the caravans. Sammy ran over. 'Anyone seen a hedgehog?' he asked.

'A hedgehog? Don't mention them! I've been *feeling* one all day and it's driving me nuts,' said one horse. This made no sense to Sammy.

Then he heard the voice again. 'I've never seen stars from this angle before.'

Sammy ran towards the voice. There was Harry, hanging upside down on a rope!

'Harry! What on earth are you doing like that?' he asked. 'Is this part of your act?'

'Some act,' said Harry. 'This is my only act now, all I'm allowed to do. I'm tied like this, swinging upside down from a carriage in order to make some horse go faster. It's the worst thing I ever heard of. Why did I join the circus? I wish I was back in the woods.'

'Well, let me untie you, and you can come home with us. We're all here,' said Sammy. Otus and Barny appeared above them as he spoke.

Harry
couldn't
believe his
eyes as the others
quickly undid the
rope. He dropped to the
ground with a smack.

'Ouch!' he said. 'Imagine! I forgot to
roll into a ball! I'll have to learn how to
be an ordinary hedgehog again.'

'Don't worry,' said Barny, 'You'll be back to your old self in no time.'

'Come on!' said Otus. 'The two of you climb on our backs and we'll get out of here.'

Sammy and Harry hopped up and the owls flapped away. The others cheered loudly when they saw Harry.

'Well, Harry, do you really want to come back to the woods with us?' asked Renny. 'Maybe you want to stay –'

'I'm coming home!' Harry butted in, and they all laughed.

Back in the woods Old Lepus and Billy Blackbird had supper ready. Harry's eyes widened when he saw all the food. 'Is it someone's birthday?' he asked.

'Well,' said Old Lepus,
'Billy flew back here to tell me
the good news. We had no
goodbye party, so we were going to
have a party to celebrate your success.
Now we'll have one to welcome you
home!'

They all cheered.

'Thank you all for getting me out of that prickly problem,' said Harry. 'Don't *ever* let me say I'm bored again.

'Let's eat,' said Old Lepus, 'and you can tell us all about life in the circus. I'm sure you were a hard act to follow.'

'You never spoke a truer word,' said Harry, as he tucked into a delicious blackberry pie.